Elizabeth Laird is the multi-award-winning author of several much-loved children's books. She has been shortlisted for the prestigious Carnegie Medal six times. She lives in Britain now, but still likes to travel as much as she can.

Also by Elizabeth Laird and published
by Macmillan Children's Books

The Fastest Boy in the World
The Prince Who Walked with Lions
The Witching Hour
Lost Riders
Crusade
Oranges in No Man's Land
Paradise End
Secrets of the Fearless
A Little Piece of Ground
The Garbage King
Jake's Tower
Red Sky in the Morning
Kiss the Dust

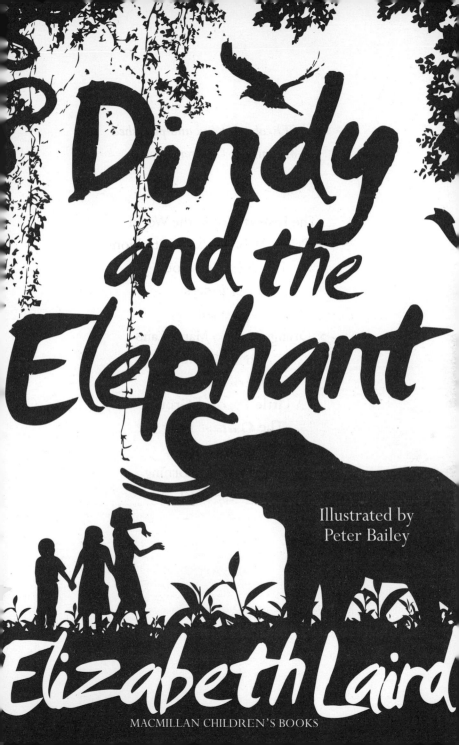

Dindy
and the
Elephant

Illustrated by
Peter Bailey

Elizabeth Laird

MACMILLAN CHILDREN'S BOOKS

First published 2015 by Macmillan Children's Books
an imprint of Pan Macmillan
20 New Wharf Road, London N1 9RR
Associated companies throughout the world
www.panmacmillan.com

ISBN 978-1-4472-8604-2 (HB)
ISBN 978-1-4472-7240-3 (PB)

1 3 5 7 9 8 6 4 2

A CIP catalogue record for this book is available from
the British Library.

Printed and bound by CPI Group (UK) Ltd, Croydon CR0 4YY

For Sam and Jack

Chapter One

'Let's play Going to England,' said Pog.

Pog's my little brother. His real name's Derek, but everyone calls him Pog. Don't ask me why. (My real name's Margaret, but everyone calls me Dindy.)

'It's silly to play Going to England,' I said. 'It's horrible there. All bombsites and rationing and fog.'

'But I *want* to,' said Pog, pushing out his lower lip in the annoying way he does when he's about to cry.

I might as well explain straight away that we live in India, in the middle of a tea plantation. Our bungalow is on a little hill with tea bushes spreading away from it all around, and jungle on the hilltops above. The nearest town is Munnar, which takes ages to get to, even on Daddy's motorbike, and our nearest English neighbours are the Richardsons, who are on the next plantation miles away. So Pog and I are on our own all the time. There's no school for British children, so Mother does our lessons at home, when she feels like it, which is hardly ever.

Pog and I had played Going to England so many times that I was fed up with it. I was nine after all, and a bit old for Let's Pretend. So I looked around, trying to think of something else to do.

Mother was resting and didn't want to be disturbed, Krishna the cook was in a bad mood as usual and would have chased us out of the kitchen, and Shanti, our ayah, who had looked after us since we were born, had gone to Munnar to get some things for Mother.

Pog was looking at me with big eyes. Once he'd thought of playing Going to England, I knew he'd go on and on about it until I gave in. All he wanted

to do was wobble about pretending to walk up the
gangway on to the ship, and go 'ooh' and 'ah' while
he watched the bit of water between the ship and
dock get wider and wider. After that, he'd spend ages
marching up and down being the ship's captain and
giving orders to the crew (me).

What Pog didn't know was that I thought
about going to England all the time. Not to pretend.
For real.

One of the main things about me is that I'm good at
keeping still and being quiet. Grown-ups often think
I'm not listening when they talk. But I *do*. And I hear
things.

A week earlier, I'd overheard a conversation that
had really made me worried.

It was just an ordinary evening except that Dr
Dysart had come over for dinner. I liked Dr Dysart.
He was always kind, even when he had to do awful
things like cutting your tonsils out. He talked in a
drawly, Scottish kind of voice. Daddy's got a Scottish
accent too, because he comes from Glasgow.

I was sitting on the window seat, as out of sight
as possible, with my legs curled up under me,
pretending to read *The Secret Garden* but really

watching everyone out of the corner of my eye and listening as hard as I could.

'The Indians will have us out of India as soon as they can,' I heard Daddy say. 'They're talking about independence everywhere. Riots, demonstrations – they'll get their way. Soon too.'

Mother's face went red. She held out her glass and shook it to make Sunderam (that's the name of our bearer) fill it up again with gin. I hate it when Mother drinks too much. She goes stupid and giggly, and then she gets cross.

'Oh, Frank,' she said, hitching up the shoulder strap of her pink satin evening gown. 'Don't be silly. If the British leave India, everything will just fall apart. You know what children the natives are.'

I looked at Sunderam's face and saw it close up. I knew what he thought of Mother. I'd often heard him and Krishna talk about her when they forgot to close the kitchen door. Pog and I can understand everything the servants say to each other. Shanti taught us their language (Malayalam) before we could even speak English.

Dr Dysart put the tips of his fingers together and looked up at the ceiling.

'I don't like to contradict you, dear lady,' he said,

'but India will do very well without the British. My own colleague, Kumar, to take one example, is an excellent doctor. Rather impressive, as a matter of fact.'

Mother's face went even redder.

'Impressive? What on earth do you mean? Native doctors are all the same. Nothing but herbs and leaves and mumbo-jumbo.'

Dr Dysart frowned.

'Dr Kumar trained in Edinburgh, and he's better qualified than I am. A fine surgeon too.' He picked up his glass and took a gulp of whisky. 'Which brings me to my own bit of news. I'm pulling out, I'm afraid. Leaving India for good. The old ticker's been playing up for a while and a quiet retirement near my daughter in Stirling is what's in store for me.'

Daddy put his own drink down on the little table beside his chair so sharply that I thought he'd cracked the glass.

'Dysart! My dear fellow! I had no idea you had a heart condition. Not too serious, I hope?'

'But you can't go, Dr Dysart! You can't!' Mother was almost shouting. 'You can't leave us here without you! How will I manage? You're the only person who understands my headaches, my spasms, my sleepless nights . . .'

I wasn't sure, but I thought that Dr Dysart was trying not to smile.

'There's nothing seriously wrong with you, Daphne, as I've told you many times. A little less gin, a little healthy exercise, some useful activity . . .'

'They'll be replacing you, I suppose?' said Daddy.

'Yes, of course.' Dr Dysart looked up at the ceiling again. 'Dr Kumar is taking over my practice. From next week, actually. He's a remarkable young man. I have every confidence in him.'

'An Indian? I wouldn't let him near me!' Mother almost shrieked. 'Frank, what are we going to do? Frank!'

Daddy shoved his chair back, scraping it noisily on the tiled floor as he stood up.

'We're going to have dinner,' he said shortly. 'Surely it's ready by now?' He turned to look at Sunderam, who was standing by the door, and was so still that he looked as if he'd been stuffed. 'Go and hurry them up in the kitchen, will you?'

Then he noticed me.

'Margaret! Why are you still up? Go and find Shanti and get her to put you to bed at once.'

I swung my legs off the window seat and went slowly towards the door, but as I opened it I heard Dr Dysart say, 'What about you and Daphne, Frank? Are you staying on? It'll be different here once the British leave. Have you thought of Kenya? I hear they're expanding the tea plantations in East Africa now.'

And Daddy said gloomily, 'No, it'll have to be England. It's time the bairns were at school. I'd try sheep farming in New Zealand, but Daphne wants London.'

As I went out, I heard Mother say crossly, 'Of course I do. After this ghastly place, I want a bit of *life*. Especially now we're being *abandoned* by our friends. I've persuaded Frank to start making enquiries at last.'

I shut the door as loudly as I dared.

Chapter Two

After I'd heard all that, it wasn't surprising that I thought about England all the time. I kept trying to imagine what it was like over there. I was born in India, and it had always been my home. Our bungalow, our garden, the trees we climbed, the bright green tea plantation stretching away on all sides, the singing of morning hymns from the Hindu temple in the valley below, the jungle-topped hills above, Krishna and Sunderam and above all Shanti — they were the whole world to me.

The thought of living in England scared me. I'd never even been there.  All I knew was that it was cold and grey and smoky, and the war had smashed everything up, and there wasn't anything nice to eat in the shops, and everyone lived in boring little boxes like the photographs of Granny's semi-detached house in Croydon, and people had to wash their own clothes and even cook their own food because there weren't any servants.

While I was thinking about all that, Pog had started kicking me on the shins.

'Come on, Dindy! Let's start. I'll let you be the captain on the ship.'

'Playing Going to England's boring,' I said. 'Let's really go somewhere. Not pretend. A real place.'

Pog looked puzzled.

'Where?'

'I don't know. Shut up and let me think.'

Pog could never do that. He can't keep quiet for a second.

'We could climb the tree outside the kitchen window again,' he said hopefully, 'and see if we can catch a chameleon.'

'Climbing that stupid tree's not going somewhere. It's still inside the garden.'

'What do you mean? We can't go outside. We're not allowed.'

But the idea of going beyond our garden fence, out into the forbidden world beyond, was sweeping me up with excitement.

'We *are* going out, though. No one will know. Mother's asleep, Daddy won't be back till late, Shanti'll be away for hours and Krishna and Sunderam are arguing in the kitchen. They won't come out till tea-time.'

Pog was biting his lip, but I could see that his eyes had gone bright, like they do before he sneaks into the kitchen to steal a biscuit when Krishna's gone to pick vegetables from the patch outside the kitchen door.

I made a sudden decision.

'We'll go down to the stream. It'll be lovely and cool down there. We can see if there are any fish.'

Pog gasped.

'The stream's miles away!'

'No, it isn't. It's only at the bottom of the hill.'

'It's really naughty to go outside without a grown-up, Dindy. You know it is.'

'And do you know something, Pog? I don't care.' I'd never felt so bold before. 'Anyway, Daddy said it was time I started making decisions and stopped being childish.'

Pog was still hesitating.

'All right.' I turned my back on him. 'I'll go on my own if you're scared.'

'I'm not scared! I'm never scared.' Pog's voice was wobbly.

I've got to admit that I was scared too, but I'd never have let him see it.

I started walking down the drive. Ram Lal, who guarded the bungalow grounds and opened and shut the gates when anyone came, was in his little house at the bottom of the drive. I knew he was always asleep in the afternoon. It would be now or never.

I heard Pog's footsteps behind me.

'I'm coming too, Dindy,' he said breathlessly.

I was relieved, to be honest. I hadn't liked the thought of going on my own.

We opened the gate quietly and slipped outside. Old Tigerlily, our dog, had been asleep under a tree. She lifted her head and whined, but when she saw it was only us, she dropped her nose on to her paws again. She'd become too old and stiff to play with us. All she could do was bark when a stranger came to the bungalow.

We stood still outside the gate for a moment and I took a deep breath. I felt almost light in the head with the daring of it. The road curved round below the wall that fenced in our garden, then it stretched away down the hill.

We'd been down that road often before, of course, but only in the car. Daddy had taken me down to the tea factory a couple of times on the back of his motorbike, and once we'd ridden on the bullock cart which had brought Shanti's family up from Munnar to visit her. But our feet had never actually walked across the ground.

'Let's go back inside, Dindy,' whispered Pog.

I nearly said yes. In fact, I was trying to think up a good reason for turning back when I heard Ram Lal cough, and then his chair shifted on the concrete floor of his gatehouse. I knew he'd come out in a minute and that he'd see us standing there.

'Come on, Pog, quick!' I grabbed Pog's hand and we began to run down the road. Behind us we heard the hinge of the gatehouse door squeak as it opened, and then there was a shout.

'Ram Lal's seen us!' panted Pog. 'We'll have to go back. He'll tell.'

'No, he won't.'

Ram Lal came from North India and spoke a different language from the other servants. He kept his distance from them, anyway. His English wasn't much good either. The only person he really talked to was Daddy, who'd been his officer in the Bengal

Lancers before we were born. They talked Bengali to each other. I knew he wouldn't tell Daddy anyway, because he'd be in trouble for being inside his house and asleep in the middle of the day.

Ram Lal was still shouting, though. It sounded like, '*Lafung! Alafung!*'

'Back soon!' I called back to him. 'We're going to meet Shanti!'

I saw him nod. He'd understood the word 'Shanti'. I could see that he thought she had given us permission. He went back inside the gates and shut them.

'Now what, Dindy?' asked Pog, who was clutching my hand tightly.

'I told you. We're going down to the stream.'

We set off again, not bothering to run any more. I felt as if I was seeing everything for the first time. The tea bushes stretching away on both sides of the track seemed a brighter green than ever before. The sky looked further away. The whole world was bigger out here. The only sound was a bird trilling away in a tree nearby.

I hadn't realized how quiet the plantation was. The silence was almost scary.

'I don't want to go to the stream,' said Pog.

'There are crocodiles down there.'

'No there aren't. The stream's not big enough for crocodiles. Who told you that, anyway?'

'Shanti.'

'She only said it to scare you so you wouldn't go down there. She says lots of things that aren't true.'

'Like what?'

'Like if you steal food and eat it, you'll get hiccups, but you're always sneaking biscuits out of the kitchen and you never get hiccups.'

Pog didn't answer. He didn't like me saying anything bad about Shanti. He loved her more than anyone else in the world. Actually, I did too, except for Daddy, but sometimes Shanti annoyed me. I'd begun to get tired of all her little rules and fusses.

We'd reached the bottom of the track that led down from the bungalow, and came out on to the wider road. Over to our right, some way away, was the huge white-painted tea factory. To our left was the village where the tea pickers and plantation workers lived.

I hesitated. If we stayed on the road, someone would be sure to come along and see us, and then we'd be in trouble.

Straight ahead, there was an opening between the

tea bushes, a path the pickers used. It led directly down the hill towards the stream. I set off down it. The bushes came up to my shoulders, and looking back I could see that they were over Pog's head. If anyone came into view, I only had to duck down and we'd both be out of sight.

I'd spent my whole life looking out across the tea garden from inside the boundary hedge of the bungalow but I'd had no idea how it felt to be in the middle of the bushes. The tea pickers worked over the bushes every morning, nipping off the new green leaves. They'd always seemed from far away to walk in a slow, comfortable sort of way. I'd always thought their work was easy. Now I realized how scratchy the bushes were, and how hot it was out in the full sun. The smell of tea was really strong too.

Behind me, Pog had started to chant his silly song, the one he does when he's upset. He doesn't know he's doing it, half the time.

> *'Diddy daddy doo,*
> *I'm not scared of you,*
> *Diddy daddy dee,*
> *I'm a great big bee.'*

He was driving me crazy. I turned on him.

'Shut up, Pog! Just – stop it!'

'Stop what?' He looked hurt.

'Your silly song.'

'What song.'

'You were doing your "Diddy Daddy".'

'No, I wasn't.'

But the words froze in my throat. Something was moving on the ground behind him, across the very bit of the path we had just come down. Something long and thin and grey, that slithered from one side of the path to the other.

I grabbed Pog's hand.

'Come on! Run!'

He tried to snatch his hand away.

'I won't. I'm going home.'

He turned as if to go back up the path.

'Pog, you can't! There's a snake. A cobra! I saw it!'

And then we were both running, crashing through the bushes, tearing our clothes, scratching our bare legs, until we almost fell out on to the wide track below that ran down to the stream.

Pog was crying.

'I told you we shouldn't have come. I *told* you!

I hate you, Dindy! We might have been bitten to death!'

'Yes, but we weren't, were we?' I was feeling so guilty that I needed to sound extra brave to cover it up. 'And it mightn't have been a cobra. It might have been one of the harmless ones.'

'No it wasn't! It was a cobra!'

'You didn't even see it, silly.'

'I want to go home!' he wailed. 'And now we

can't, because there are cobras all over the path!'

'We won't have to go back that way, through the tea. We'll go round by the road.'

'I want to go *now*!' Pog's wails were getting louder, but I was full of triumph. We'd escaped from home, braved a snake and seen it off, and we were nearly down as far as the stream. I wasn't going to let a snivelling little boy spoil everything now.

Then I heard them. Children's voices. Shouts and laughter.

'I caught it! It's mine!' one of them was squealing. 'Give it back!'

'I'm going to see what they've caught,' I said to Pog, slipping out of English into Malayalam.

Pog stopped crying and stared at me.

'We're not allowed to play with native children,' he said in English. You know we're not. Only with Nikhil.'

Nikhil was Shanti's son. He was two years older than me and we'd known him forever. When he was smaller, he'd often come to the house with Shanti, and played with us.

'You know we're not allowed,' Pog said again.

I'd suddenly run right out of patience with him. I couldn't stand his whining any longer.

'If you don't want to come, don't,' I said brutally. 'Find your own way home.'

And without looking back I ran down the last stretch of track to the bank above the stream.

Chapter Three

There were only six or seven boys at the water's edge, but they looked like a crowd to me. They stared at me open-mouthed as I scrambled down the bank to join them. They were standing quite still, and I suddenly felt shy.

'Hello,' I said. 'Did you catch a fish? Can I see it?'

One of them nudged another and said, 'Did you hear that? She speaks Malayalam.'

'I told you she did,' said a gruff voice.

I hadn't seen Nikhil. He'd been squatting on a stone beside the fast-running water. He was holding a fish and scraping the scales off it with a stone. I felt a surge of relief that he was there. I wished he'd stand up and look at me, but he just went on scraping at the fish.

The boys were edging away from me.

'We weren't doing anything,' said one.

'Is your father with you?' said another.

Why are they scared of me? I thought.

I smiled, trying to look friendly. 'No. He's away till tonight. I just wanted to . . . I heard you and . . .'

I stopped. I didn't like the way they were looking at me.

Nikhil stood up at last. I hadn't seen him for months, and he'd grown. He towered over me now.

'Where's Pog?'

'I don't know. I . . .'

My face was growing red. I'd suddenly realized that I'd abandoned my little brother in the middle of the tea plantation, with goodness knows how many cobras crawling around in the bushes, and he didn't even know how to find his way home.

'I'll go and find him,' I said, turning to run off.

'No need!' a boy called out. 'There he is.'

Pog must have followed me. He was standing at the top of the bank. He looked awful. His face was scratched and smeared with mud and tears, his shorts were torn and there were twigs in his hair.

One of the boys sniggered.

'Little sahib looks like a street kid,' I heard him say.

'We were coming down through the tea bushes,' I said defensively. 'I saw a cobra. We had to run.'

Nikhil frowned.

'You shouldn't have gone through the tea. We never do. You can damage the bushes.'

I felt humiliated. Not even the cobra had impressed Nikhil, and now he was telling me off in front of these boys. Mother would be furious. She thought that all Indians ought to treat us with respect.

'We can do what we like,' Pog called out aggressively. 'The bushes belong to our daddy.'

He scrambled down the bank and stood beside me.

'No, they don't,' the biggest boy said, stepping forward till he was quite close. 'The plantation belongs to the company. Your father's only the manager.'

The spell that had kept them quiet seemed to have been broken.

'And he won't be much longer when India gets independence!' another boy called out.

I felt Pog's hand slide into mine, and I was glad of it.

'What's independence, Dindy?' he whispered.

'I'll tell you later,' I whispered back, though I wasn't sure myself.

The boys had gained confidence now. They came closer, crowding round us.

'There won't be any white sahibs in India any more,' one of them said. 'We're going to be our own bosses now.'

I felt Pog stiffen.

'You can't be,' he said hotly. 'Natives are like children. Mummy says so. Children can't be bosses.'

'Pog!' I hissed. 'Shut up!'

There was shock and anger on the faces around me. Then, which was worse, they looked as if they were going to laugh.

'Listen to the little sahib!' one of them jeered.

Another snatched the fish out of Nikhil's hand and dangled it in front of Pog's face.

'You British are finished here. Dead. Like this fish.'

I felt really frightened now.

'Please don't be angry with him,' I said. 'He's only six.'

'Let him fight his own battles,' a boy at the back called out. 'Look at him! He can't wait to grow up and be like his daddy and rule over us. He can't wait to take all our money out of our country!'

Nikhil stepped up to stand beside me.

'Come on, Dindy. I'll take you home. You shouldn't have come here. Don't you know it's dangerous to be out in the tea garden today?'

I didn't like the way he was trying to sound like a grown-up.

'We can manage, thank you.' I was being as dignified as I could. 'I know the way home. We'll go round by the road.'

'No!' he looked exasperated. 'You don't understand. Haven't you heard about the elephant?'

'What elephant?' said Pog eagerly, forgetting that he was offended.

The other boys had quietened down. They were nodding.

'Nikhil's right,' one of them said. 'There's a rogue male. A wild tusker. He came out of the jungle last night. He's been rampaging around the tea garden all day. Didn't you wonder why the tea pickers weren't out today?'

'If you meet him, he'll go for you,' said another.

'Trample you to death.' The boy who'd said that was grinning.

Pog's hand was gripping mine so hard that it hurt. I could tell that he was trying not to cry. I was having to keep a hold of myself too, actually, to keep the tears out of my eyes.

'Why didn't Ram Lal warn you?' said Nikhil. 'He should never have let you out of the gate.'

'He was asleep in his house. He . . .' And then I remembered. Ram Lal had shouted, '*Lafung! Alafung!*' He must have been trying to say 'elephant' in English. 'We told him we were going to meet Shanti,' I said, knowing that it sounded bad.

'My mother's in Munnar. You know she is.' Nikhil sounded sterner than ever. 'You'll get Ram Lal into terrible trouble.'

I stared at him, feeling awful.

'What are we going to do?' I whispered.

'Don't ask him!' one of the boys shouted. 'He's only a native. A child. Ask your little sahib. He'll tell you what to do.'

'Shut up, funny boy,' said Nikhil. He was chewing his lip, thinking. 'Look, we'll go along the stream to the depot. The plantation elephants came in from the next valley this morning. Their keeper will know what to do. It's safe to go along the bank. Wild elephants never come this far downhill. Now stick beside me, and don't make a noise. That goes for you too, Pog. Do you understand?'

Pog nodded.

'Come on, then.'

And, following Nikhil, we set off along the side of the stream.

Chapter Four

The path that ran beside the stream was narrow, and we had to go round boulders and jump over the roots of big trees that leaned out across the water. It was shady and cool here. The only sound was the buzzing of flies and the gurgling of water in the stream, which had widened out so that it was more like a small river. I'd never been so close to it before.

It's really nice down here, I thought. The idea of the wild elephant didn't seem so frightening in this quiet, peaceful place.

I kept looking sideways at Nikhil as we walked along. He was grimly silent, going fast and looking straight ahead.

'You don't come and play with us any more,' I said at last.

'No time. I'm at secondary school now. Didn't you know?'

'Oh. I suppose I did.'

I must have sounded disappointed because he

looked down at me and said, 'I used to like playing with all your toys. Especially the rocking horse. I didn't have anything like that at home.'

'Oh,' I said again.

I had a horrible thought. Had Nikhil only ever wanted to be with us because of our toys? It was true that he had preferred to play alone, without our interference. He'd always been quiet, and had let us boss him around, even though he was so much older than we were. Had we – had I – been nasty to him?

'I liked it when you came,' I said anxiously. 'You used to make funny faces. They made Pog laugh. And me too.'

At last, Nikhil smiled.

'Yes. He was really sweet when he was little.'

But not sweet any more, I could almost hear him think.

He was walking so fast that I had to hurry to keep up, and Pog was almost running behind us.

'When did the tusker come?' I asked, trying to think of something to say. 'Was it this morning?'

'During the night.'

'Did he hurt anyone?'

Nikhil actually grinned.

'He chased the foreman right in through the

factory gates. They only just closed them in time.'

I'd met the foreman once when Daddy had taken me to the factory. He was quite fat and short, and he shouted at the workmen, but when he talked to Daddy he smiled and smiled and waggled his head till I thought it would drop off. The thought of him being chased by an elephant, his short legs pumping along as fast they could, was so funny that I laughed out loud. Nikhil laughed too.

I took a deep breath.

'Pog didn't mean to be rude to those boys, Nikhil.'

The smile dropped off Nikhil's face.

'No. He can't help himself. It's the way he's been taught to think.'

'I don't think . . . like that.'

He frowned down at me.

'You don't think that Indians are all children? You don't think that you British are born to rule?'

I said nothing. I'd never thought about it at all.

'I don't know,' I said.

'You don't *know* anything, Dindy. Nothing about us. Nothing about this country. You live up there, in your bungalow, with all your beautiful toys, and Krishna, and Sunderam, and Ram Lal, and *my mother* . . .'

There was a knot in my throat.

'I really love Shanti,' I said. 'Better than anyone.'

'So do I, Dindy, but she's spent far more time with you than she ever could with me.'

I'd never thought of that before.

'I'm sorry,' I whispered.

'It's not your fault,' he said gruffly. 'You're a nice kid. You just don't know anything, that's all. You'd better start knowing, though, because once we get our independence . . .'

There was a yelp behind us. We turned, and saw that Pog had stumbled over the huge root of a tree that had made a hump in the path. Blood oozed from a cut on his knee. He got to his feet and looked down at it, biting back tears.

'It's not too bad, Dindy,' he said. 'It doesn't hurt too much.'

'He's brave – I'll say that for him,' said Nikhil. 'Come on, Pog. We're nearly there. You'd better hold my hand.'

The depot was a large open space, set a little way back from the stream and surrounded by tall trees. There was a big shed where the estate's two lorries were kept, and a pile of rusting old machinery. The four working elephants were standing in the shade. They were chained by the back legs to huge posts. They stood quite still, their trunks limp and drooping, as if they were resting. Only their ears flapped from time to time as they tried to shake off the flies that buzzed around their eyes.

Pog and I had seen the estate's tame working elephants quite often before. They weren't usually at this end of the tea plantation, but sometimes, when they were, Daddy would drive us down in his car as a treat to look at them. We'd even ridden on an old one once. I'd been a bit scared of falling off, but Pog had loved it. He'd shouted so loudly that the mahout (the man who looked after the elephants) had to tell Daddy to keep him quiet in case the elephant got upset.

There didn't seem to be anyone around. Now that Nikhil had taken charge of us, I'd half forgotten the trouble we were in, but when I saw that the mahout wasn't there I started to get worried again.

'Why don't we shout and see if anyone will come?' I said.

'You don't want to scare the elephants,' said Nikhil. 'And, anyway, we don't shout. It's rude.'

I bit my lip. Daddy was always shouting at people. Mother shouted at Sunderam all the time too.

Nikhil cleared his throat loudly, and then I saw the mahout. He was standing quite still in the shade behind the elephants. He wore only a brown cloth, which was wrapped round his waist and pulled up between his legs, like bulky shorts. His dark skin was almost the same colour as the trunks of the trees that surrounded him.

Nikhil went towards him.

'Hello, sir,' he said politely. 'Are you well?'

The mahout stepped out of the shade, and moved his head from side to side in a silent greeting.

'Why sahib's children here?'

He spoke a funny kind of Malayalam. He was one of the hill people, Daddy had said, who had their own language. They'd lived for hundreds of years in the forest, and understood more about wild animals in general and elephants in particular than anyone else in India. That was why they were such good mahouts.

'The children came out on their own. They were naughty. Now they must go home,' Nikhil said slowly, making sure he could understand.

The mahout didn't look at us. His eyes narrowed against the sun as he stared out beyond the clearing up the hillside of tea bushes towards where our bungalow could just be seen, far above, as if it was floating in another world.

'Rogue tusker,' he said. 'Not safe.'

My heart sank.

'Please,' I said, speaking slowly in Malayalam like Nikhil. 'Can't you help us?'

I'd been holding Pog's hand, but now he shook it free and crossed his arms.

'You must,' he said loudly in Malayalam. 'You've got to take us home.'

He looked and sounded just like Daddy. I snatched his hand back.

'Shut up, you little idiot,' I said in English. 'Don't shout. It's rude.'

'I wasn't shouting. I was just telling him.'

'We've got to ask nicely.'

'Why? Daddy doesn't.'

'You're not Daddy. If you want to get home, just keep quiet.'

Nikhil and the mahout were still talking.

'Cannot take children,' the mahout was saying. 'Cannot leave my elephants here. If tusker comes, they are too upset. Break free.'

'I can take them, Father!'

A boy had come up from the stream. He was dressed like the mahout, barefoot, with only a cloth round his waist, and he was shiny with water, as if he'd been bathing.

'Hello, Nikhil,' he said.

'Silveraj!' said Nikhil. 'I haven't seen you for ages.'

'Not since you went to your fancy secondary school.' The boy grinned. He spoke good Malayalam, like Nikhil. 'How did these two precious little whiteys get out of their prison up there? Are you leading them astray? Your mum won't like it.'

'It's not Nikhil's fault,' I said quickly. 'It was me.'

Silveraj's mouth dropped open.

'She speaks Malayalam?' he said to Nikhil, as if he still didn't think I could understand. 'Where did she learn it?'

'From my mother, of course,' Nikhil said shortly. 'Look, can you really take them home? I've got to get back to the village before my grandmother starts making a fuss.'

Silveraj looked at his father.

'Not safe,' the mahout grunted again. 'Rogue tusker.'

'But I can do that thing, Father, like you showed me, if he comes,' Silveraj said eagerly.

'Do what?' asked Nikhil.

Silveraj ignored him. He was still watching his father's face.

There was a long pause. Then the mahout walked over to where the elephants were chained. Fresh balls of steaming dung, as big as loaves of bread, were piled

behind each animal. The mahout jerked his chin at Silveraj, who ran across to him, then he bent down, scooped up some dung with his hand and smeared it on Silveraj's back and chest.

'Look, Dindy! That's disgusting! That's elephant's big jobs!' squealed Pog delightedly.

'I've heard of mahouts doing that,' said Nikhil. 'It's clever. If the tusker comes, he won't smell Silveraj like a boy. He'll think he's another elephant. He won't get angry.'

Pog shook my hand off.

'Put some on me!' he called out, much too loudly, and he ran over to the elephants.

The mahout said something angrily to Silveraj.

'He says you've got to be quiet, and not jump around, or he won't let me go,' Silveraj warned Pog, then he picked up some dung and smeared it on Pog's arms.

'On Dindy too,' said Pog, in what he thought was a whisper.

He scooped up some dung, and ran across to me. I shrank back.

'No, thanks.'

'You must, Dindy, or the elephant'll go for you,' squealed Pog, lunging forward with his handful of dung. I dived behind Nikhil. Pog dodged round after me, half choking with laughter.

'Be *quiet*,' Nikhil was saying, but he was laughing too.

Pog won, and I ended up with streaks of tawny-coloured elephant dung along my arms. It wasn't nearly as nasty as I'd thought it would be. It smelled of freshly baked bread, and didn't seem dirty at all.

Silveraj came up to us.

'My father says I can take you home, but only if you promise to be quiet and do everything I say.'

'But . . .' began Pog.

Nikhil bent down, picked him up, and held him inches away from his face.

'No buts, Pog. No little-sahib stuff now. It's dangerous. Silveraj knows what to do. You don't. If you don't behave yourself, you'll put all three of you in danger. You don't want Dindy to get hurt, do you? Now. Are you going to be good?'

I saw Pog swallow.

'Yes, Nikhil.'

Nikhil set him down again.

'Goodbye, then. You'll be all right if you do what you're told. Silveraj will see you safe home.'

'Aren't you coming with us, Nikhil?' I said, my

voice sounding small even to me.

'No. I've got to get back to the village. I told you.'

'But will you be safe? What if you meet the elephant yourself?'

'It's not far. I'll keep close to the stream. I'll go quickly and be quiet.'

I hated seeing him go. I darted forward and flung my arms round him.

'Thank you, Nikhil, and I'm sorry.'

'What for?'

'*Everything*,' I said.

Chapter Five

The sunlight was so bright when we stepped out of the shade that I had to blink and screw up my eyes. That's when I realized that I had lost my hat.

'You've lost your hat, Dindy,' Pog said annoyingly.

'So what? You've lost yours.'

I was trying to sound as if I didn't care, but I knew that losing our hats would make the trouble we were in even worse. We were never allowed to go outside, even into our garden, without our hats on.

'You'll get heatstroke,' Mother would say. 'And sunburn. And fevers. And eyestrain.'

I could feel the hot sun burning through my hair already.

Silveraj was walking ahead of us. He was going fast, but in a smooth way. It was as if he was almost floating, his bare feet making no noise on the loose stones of the track.

I took Pog's hand.

'Come on. You've got to keep up.'

'I can't, Dindy. I'm really, really tired. And thirsty. Are we going to be late for tea?'

Silveraj turned when he heard us talking and waited for us to catch him up.

'If the tusker comes,' he said, 'you have to run downhill, into the tea. Elephants don't like going down steep slopes.'

'We can't,' objected Pog. 'There are snakes in there.'

'Never mind the snakes. There are no poisonous ones, anyway.'

'There are,' I said. 'We saw a cobra on the way down. A really long one.'

'Did you see its head?'

'No.'

'Then how do you know it was a cobra?'

'We just . . .'

'And if it was a cobra,' Silveraj went on, 'then you were lucky.'

'Lucky? It might have bitten us to death!'

'The cobra is a powerful god. He'll protect you if you pray to him and respect him.'

'Pray to a cobra?' I was shocked. 'Cobras aren't gods. Jesus is the only god. Our vicar says that all the other ones are heathen idols.'

I didn't know the words in Malayalam so I said them in English.

'What do you mean, "hea-ten idles"? I don't know those words,' said Silveraj. 'It doesn't matter, anyway. Jesus is a very good god. Like Krishna, and Vishnu . . .'

I felt my face growing hot.

'Jesus isn't like – like . . .'

'Dindy,' said Pog. 'I've got a stone in my shoe.'

I bent down to take his sandal off and shake the stone out, grateful to Pog for interrupting. I hadn't known how to answer Silveraj. By the time I stood up, he'd lost interest in gods anyway.

We set off along the track. Silveraj had been talking softly, but in a normal way, and everything looked so ordinary, so quiet and peaceful, that it was impossible to imagine that an elephant would appear. Birds were singing as usual in the few trees that were dotted about among the tea bushes, and from the workers' village below I could hear cows mooing.

'Nikhil says you've got a cupboard full of clothes just for you,' Silveraj said curiously. 'And there's another one for the boy.'

I couldn't see what was strange about that.

'Of course I have,' I said.

'And there's a room where you sleep on your own. Aren't you frightened? What happens if a ghost comes?'

'Daddy says there's no such thing as ghosts. And if I have a bad dream and wake up, Shanti comes and sings me back to sleep.'

'Why doesn't your mother come?'

'Her bedroom's too far away. She can't hear me.'

It wasn't the real reason, I knew. Mother hated being disturbed when she was asleep. Anyway, it was Shanti's soft arms I wanted around me, and her crooning voice I wanted to hear when I felt the fear of the night.

'Your brother's got a bicycle, hasn't he? A little one, especially for a child.'

'Yes.'

Silveraj's questions were making me feel more and more uncomfortable. To stop them, I thought of one myself.

'How did you get to be friends with Nikhil?'

'How do you think? We were in the same class in primary school. He's lucky. His mother's got a good job so she can pay for him to go to secondary school. My father can't afford to send me.'

I nearly said, 'Shanti doesn't have a job,' and then

I realized that she did have one. It was looking after Pog and me. I'd never thought of it as a 'job' before.

'After independence, when you British go, Shanti will lose her job and Nikhil will have to leave school,' Silveraj said casually.

I felt as if he'd hit me.

No! I was screaming in my head. *Shanti won't lose her job! She'll come to England with us. She must! I can't manage without her!*

'You don't go to school, do you?' Silveraj's quiet voice went on. 'Don't your parents care about your education?'

'Mother teaches us.' I'd started detesting Silveraj. I wanted to hit him and run away. 'And we'll go to boarding school in England when we're older.'

'My father wouldn't want me to go away anywhere.' He sounded hatefully proud. 'He's training me to be a mahout.'

'Lucky you,' I said, and then I felt tears well up in my eyes, and before I could stop them, they were running down my cheeks.

Silveraj noticed.

'Don't cry, little girl. What's the matter?'

'I don't want to go to England!' I burst out. 'I don't want to leave home here, and – and India.

I want to be friends with Nikhil again, only he doesn't like us any more. And I can't live without Shanti. I can't!'

We'd stopped walking in the middle of the road. Silveraj looked confused.

'But you must be so happy up there in your big house, with all your money, and cupboards full of clothes, and hundreds of toys and plenty of food and your mother and father. If I was you, I'd be so happy I'd burst.'

'No, you wouldn't.' I wiped my arm along my nose, forgetting about the elephant dung. 'It's not like that at all.'

I'd surprised Silveraj, I could tell. He was looking at me as if he'd never seen me before.

'You're the first British person I've ever talked to,' he said. 'I've only ever seen you people from a distance, in your cars, or up there behind the fence in your garden, or your father on his motorbike coming to give orders to mine. You're not like I expected.'

We'd reached the first bend in the road, and the start of the track that led to the bungalow. It zig-zagged up the steep slope, turning one sharp corner after another.

It was harder work now that we were going uphill and Pog was going more and more slowly.

'Stop, Dindy!' he panted, after we'd gone round the first bend. 'I've got another stone in my sandal.'

I could tell he was making it up.

'No, you haven't. You just wanted to stop for a rest,' I said crossly.

'Honestly, I have, Dindy. Take my sandal off and look.'

I bent down again, but before I'd undone the buckle I felt Silveraj's hand pressing down urgently on my shoulder.

'Stand up slowly, very slowly,' he said quietly. 'Don't make a sound or move suddenly.'

Pog was looking over my head.

'It's the elephant, Dindy!' he shrieked. 'It's coming! It's right there in front of us! I'm scared!'

I was on my feet again at once. Silveraj pushed me in the back.

'Get down into the tea. Take him with you. Be quick. Go down the steepest bit.'

'Cobras!' wailed Pog.

'No cobras. Go on! Now!'

I grabbed Pog's arm and then we were both scrambling madly down through the tea bushes, ignoring the scratches on our arms and legs, while behind us came the most terrifying sound I had ever heard in my life, the screaming trumpet of a wild, angry elephant.

Chapter Six

I seemed to go crashing on down through the tea bushes forever. The terrified pounding of my heart was so loud in my ears that I was sure it must be echoing all over the plantation. I'd forgotten all about Pog. I was sure that the sound of breaking twigs behind me was the noise of the elephant, right on my heels.

And then I tripped and fell, and before I could get up again, Pog had fallen on top of me, flattening me to the ground. I struggled to sit up.

Pog was whimpering. His eyes were wide with fear and his face, under the scratches and layers of dirt and dung, was a horrible white colour.

'I've wet myself, Dindy. I couldn't help it. The elephant's going to kill me, isn't he?'

I'd nearly always found Pog infuriating, babyish, silly and selfish, but I suddenly realized that I loved my brother. I gave him a hug with my shaking arms.

'I don't know, Pog. He doesn't seem to be after us

right now. I'm really sorry. I shouldn't have brought you out with me.'

He shook me off.

'Take a look, Dindy, and see where he is.'

I got to my knees, trying not to rustle a single leaf, and slowly lifted my head above the bushes. There was no elephant behind us, and for a moment I thought that he and Silveraj had disappeared, and that I'd imagined the whole thing.

Then I saw them, the elephant and the boy. They were walking calmly side by side up the track. They reached the place where the path led off the track up the hill towards the forest far above, and I breathed out with relief as Silveraj turned along it. He didn't even look back. He knew the elephant would follow him, and it did.

'You can get up, Pog. Look.'

We stood there, awe-struck, our two blond heads sticking out above the sea of brilliant green bushes, watching silently. Silveraj was walking at the same quiet, even pace as the elephant, measuring him step with step. He seemed almost to glide. His arms hung down by his sides, and as he walked they swayed, just like the elephant's trunk.

'Look, Pog. He's being an elephant himself.

He saved us. He saved our lives.'

Pog tugged at my skirt.

'Can we go home now, Dindy? Please?'

'In a minute. We'd better let them get further away first.'

At that moment, I became aware of an engine, roaring away in the distance. It was coming closer and closer. Then I realized what it was. A motorbike.

'Daddy! Daddy's coming!' yelled Pog, and before I could stop him, he was charging back up through the tea bushes and had tumbled out on to the track above.

I followed him slowly. I wanted Daddy to be there, so safe and strong, but I was scared too. I was going to be in terrible trouble. There was no chance of slipping quietly back into our garden. We'd been out much longer than I'd intended.

It wasn't the beating I'd get that I dreaded so much as the anger and disappointment in Daddy's face. Mother wouldn't hit me, but she'd be even angrier, and say horrible things.

I'd have to face them sooner or later. Reluctantly I went out on to the track and stood waiting beside Pog while the sound of the motorbike came closer and closer.

It rounded the bend and skidded to a halt.

'It's not Daddy! It's not!' Pog cried out, and burst into tears, big noisy sobs that shook his whole body.

The biker took off his helmet. He was Indian, but he looked different, somehow, from the Indians we knew. He wore a white cotton suit and a tie, like Daddy's.

'You must be the Fraser children,' he said. 'What are you doing out here? Is everything all right?'

He spoke English without an accent, as if he was English himself.

Pog was crying too hard to answer. The man was

staring at us, astonished, and I suddenly realized how dreadful we looked. Our faces were smeared with tears and filth, our hair was matted and wild, our clothes were torn, blood was oozing from the scratches on our arms and legs, and the front of Pog's shorts was soaked with pee.

'How – how do you do?' I said, trying to sound grown up. 'Who are you?'

'I'm your new doctor. Dr Kumar. I've come to see your mother and father. You're going to be my patients.'

Pog stopped crying as suddenly as he'd started.

'You're not a doctor. You're an Indian.'

Dr Kumar smiled.

'I'm an Indian *and* I'm a doctor.'

This didn't satisfy Pog.

'Indians are supposed to talk Malayalam. Why are you talking English?'

'I can speak Malayalam if you like,' said Dr Kumar. 'Shall we discuss it later? You children look as if you've been in the wars. Do you want me to take you home?'

'Yes!' burst out Pog. 'Oh, yes!'

He was already running to the bike, his arms held out, waiting to be helped up on to it.

I hung back.

'We're not supposed to go anywhere with strangers,' I said.

'Quite right. But I'm your new doctor, so we won't be strangers much longer. Didn't Dr Dysart tell your father?'

I nodded unwillingly.

'Take Pog,' I said. 'I'll walk.'

Dr Kumar sat back on the saddle of the bike, one hand resting on the handlebars, like a picture of a film star in one of Mother's magazines.

'What's happened, Margaret? Your name is Margaret, isn't it? Do you want to tell me before I take you home?'

He sounded so kind and gentle that I wanted to cry too. I would have sobbed as loudly as Pog if I hadn't made a huge effort to stop myself.

'It's all my fault!' I blurted out. 'I wanted to explore. I made Pog come too. And there was a snake in the tea, and Nikhil doesn't like me any more, and the elephant came and we thought he was going to kill us. And when we go home everyone's going to be furious with me, and Daddy's going to beat me with his slipper.'

Dr Kumar seemed to be having problems understanding me.

'Did you say an elephant?' he said at last. 'What elephant?'

'A wild one. A tusker,' said Pog, who was already climbing up to sit in front of Dr Kumar behind the handlebars. 'Silveraj took it away.'

Dr Kumar was looking more and more bewildered.

'It was going to attack us,' I explained. 'And Silveraj, he's the mahout's son, he just walked away with it. Look. You can still see them. He's taking the elephant out of the tea garden into the jungle.'

Dr Kumar followed my pointing finger. Silveraj and the elephant were high up the hill by now, though still some way from the edge of the forest. They were walking steadily side by side, keeping to the same quiet, easy pace, as if they had been friends forever.

'That's a wild elephant?' said Dr Kumar.

'Yes.'

He let out a whistle.

'That's the most remarkable thing I've seen in my whole life. The bravest thing I've ever heard of.'

He watched Silveraj for a moment or two longer, then turned back to us.

'Come on, young lady,' he said. 'Let's take you home. Hop up behind me and hold on tight. You can't put it off forever. It's time to face the music.'

We were much nearer home than I'd thought we were, and it was only a few minutes later when Dr Kumar pulled his bike up outside the gates.

Ram Lal ran to open them. He looked shocked and relieved at the same time to see us, and he started speaking fast and loudly in his own language. Dr Kumar seemed to understand, and said something that calmed Ram Lal down a bit, and then he drove right to the front porch, and pulled up at the bottom of the steps to the front door. Pog tumbled off the bike and ran up the steps, straight into Mother, who was coming out.

I could tell at once that it was going to be bad. Mother was red in face and she had to put her hand on one of the pillars of the porch to steady herself.

'What's all this?' she shouted, her voice thick. 'You wicked child! You . . .' But then she was looking over my head and glaring at Dr Kumar. 'Who the hell are you? Where did you take my daughter? What have you done to her?'

Dr Kumar went up the steps towards her with his hand held out, ready to shake hers.

'It's all right, Mrs Fraser. I found the children—'
But Mother slapped his hand away furiously.

'Don't you dare touch me! Who do you think you are?'

I couldn't bear to hear any more. I put my hands over my ears and ran up the steps, ducking to avoid the blow she aimed at me. I raced down the corridor to my room, calling out, 'Shanti! Shanti! Where are you?'

Shanti was always at our end of the corridor at that time of day, but she wasn't there now. I flung myself down on my bed. I couldn't even cry. There was a horrible knot inside me, and all I could do was put my pillow over my head to blot out the sound of Mother shouting, wishing that everything would go away.

Chapter Seven

It seemed like ages, but actually I don't think it was very long before I heard the roar of another motorbike, loud enough to come through the pillow. I took the pillow off my head and sat up.

Daddy, I thought, my eyes squeezed tight with dread.

The engine cut out. Mother was still screeching, and I knew she was saying terrible things. Then I heard Daddy's voice, sharp with anger.

'Daphne! What is this? You're hysterical. Dr Kumar, I'm so sorry. *Daphne!* Shut up!'

Then, unbelievably, there was the sound of a slap, and Mother's voice was cut off in mid-word. I heard the clatter of her high heels staggering along the corridor to her bedroom at the far end of the bungalow, and a bang as she slammed her door.

I got up, crept to the door of my room and opened it a crack, desperate to hear what Dr Kumar would say. Daddy was taking him into his den, the little room nearly opposite my bedroom, where he always went to write his letters. I heard chairs scrape on the wooden floor as they sat down.

'Look,' Daddy said, his voice tense with embarrassment, 'I honestly don't know what to say.'

'She certainly . . . let rip,' Dr Kumar said stiffly. 'I know that's what you people think of us, but I've never heard it expressed so . . . bluntly before.'

Daddy cleared his throat.

'I don't share my wife's views, I can assure you, Doctor. I don't know why you should believe me, but . . .' His voice tailed off.

There was a long silence. I started to feel a glimmer of hope.

Perhaps Dr Kumar won't tell about finding us outside, I thought. *And Mother might be too far gone to remember too.*

'Actually, I do believe you,' Dr Kumar said at last, his voice a shade warmer. 'Dr Dysart has briefed me fairly thoroughly on the attitudes of my future patients.'

'Dr Dysart,' said Daddy, glad to have found a neutral subject. 'A good man, that. He speaks very highly of you.'

They were silent again. My hopes began to rise.

'She — she's not happy, you see,' Daddy said, sounding almost pleading. 'India doesn't suit her. She never feels well. She has these . . . these episodes from time to time. She'll be better when we're back in England.'

'Yes.'

Silence again.

Don't say anything! Don't tell him! I was silently praying, my fists balled into tight knots.

'What brought it all on, anyway?' asked Daddy, making my stomach jump with fright. 'Daphne didn't just launch in at the sight of you, I hope? Didn't I hear her say something about the children?'

'Yes. I found them some way down the lane, on their own.' I couldn't believe how calmly Dr Kumar spoke as he betrayed us. 'They seem to have had some kind of adventure.'

'What? The children were out of the compound? Without an adult? Why on earth . . . ?'

I couldn't bear to listen any longer. I shut the door as quietly as I could, ran back to my bed and pressed the pillow over my head again. I was so anxious I thought I was going to be sick.

At last the door opened. I coiled myself into a ball with my face turned to the wall.

'What have you been doing? Dindy! Look at me!'

It wasn't Daddy's dreaded voice, but Shanti's dear one.

I flew off the bed and ran towards her, wanting to wrap my arms round her waist. But to my horror she backed away from me.

'How could you do such a thing, Dindy? You are a very, very naughty girl. To go out like that! And take Pog into danger! As soon as my back was turned!'

'Shanti,' I said desperately. 'Please don't be cross. I'm so sorry. I didn't . . .'

But Shanti's voice was hardening.

'No sorry, sorry, Shanti. Now Ram Lal is in bad trouble, and so am I, and Dr Kumar is getting all the blame, and look at you! Filthy! And your good skirt torn to pieces!'

She grabbed my arm in a fierce grip. She'd never touched me so unkindly before in my whole life.

'Get into the bathroom. Now. Take a bath. You can run it yourself for a change. I'm not going to be your servant any more when you go home to England. You might as well get used to looking after yourself.'

She was dragging me to the door and down the corridor to the bathroom.

I wanted to shout back at her, cry, plead, do anything to bring her back to her usual self, but I was afraid I would only make things worse.

'Shanti, I'm sorry, I'm sorry, please, Shanti,' was all I could say, and then I was in the bathroom and a towel was thrust into my hand, my pyjamas and slippers were dumped on the floor, and the door shut with a snap behind me.

I know this must sound feeble, but I'd never given myself a bath before. Shanti had always run the water for me, laid out the soap and towels, helped me out of my clothes, folded them and taken them away to be washed. I didn't know what to do. I'd found her irritating, sometimes, the way she'd fussed over me, but I'd have given anything to have her looking after me now. I slid down on to the mat beside the bath and sat there helplessly, crying.

Down the corridor, I could hear Pog talking, his voice squeaky with excitement, and Shanti sounding like herself, soothing and kind. I knew she was tutting at his scratches, and telling him what a brave boy he'd been. I knew he was heaping all the blame on me.

After a while, Shanti came back. She stood there, frowning down at me. Then she sighed, put the plug into the bath, turned the taps on and began to tug at my clothes. I didn't dare say anything, but just tried to control the hiccups my sobs had brought on.

'Get in and wash yourself,' she said at last, when the bath was ready, and went out again.

I scrubbed myself hard all over, going at the smears of elephant dung with the nailbrush until my arms were red and sore. Then I got out, dried myself as best I could, and struggled into my pyjamas.

I sat on the edge of the bath, not knowing what to do next. When she came back in, she said nothing, but filled the basin with water, reached for the shampoo on the high shelf above it, and pushed my head down.

I hate having my hair washed, and I'd always made a fuss about it. But this time I didn't even squirm. Shanti's hands were rougher than usual as she massaged the shampoo into my scalp, not caring if she tore at the knots, and the water she tipped over my head to rinse it was too hot. I didn't make a sound, but kept as still as I could, even though the shampoo had got into my eyes and was making them sting furiously.

But once she'd wrapped the towel round my head, and saw how red my eyes were, with the shampoo foam still in the corners, her face softened a bit, and she wiped my face.

'Shanti, I . . .' I began, wanting to start saying sorry all over again, but before I could begin I heard voices in the corridor outside. Daddy was saying goodbye to Dr Kumar, and their footsteps were going away towards the front door.

I imagined Dr Kumar climbing on to his motorbike, and waited for the roar of the engine as he kick-started it.

Now I'm for it, I thought. *Daddy'll come now.*

He was on his way back towards us. I could

hear him. I clung tightly to Shanti.

'Don't let him beat me! Please, Shanti!'

But then his footsteps stopped. There was a noise of doors opening, and voices calling urgently from the far end of the bungalow.

'Dr Sahib! Doctor! Don't go!' Sunderam was shouting. 'Mem Sahib is ill. Really ill. She needs you, Doctor! Now!'

Chapter Eight

I ran to the bathroom door and looked along the corridor. Dr Kumar was arguing with Daddy by the front door.

'She won't accept my help — you know that,' he was saying. 'Accept the truth, Mr Fraser. She's drunk. Let her sleep it off.'

'Dr Sahib! Come now!' Sunderam called out.

'Please,' begged Daddy. 'Just look at her. Please.'

Dr Kumar hesitated. Then he shrugged his shoulders.

'If you insist. Get your bearer to fetch my bag from the pannier on my bike. And I'll need a woman with me if I'm to examine her.'

'A woman?' Daddy ran his fingers through his hair. 'There isn't . . .'

'Haven't your children got an ayah?'

'Shanti! Of course!'

Shanti was already pushing me aside and running towards him.

'Look after Pog!' she called to me over her shoulder.

I stood in the corridor and watched as she disappeared into Mother's bedroom. Then I saw Sunderam run back into the house with Dr Kumar's big black bag, and Krishna came hurrying out of the kitchen with a bowl and towels and a jug of steaming water. And then, with Mother's door shut, there was silence.

I heard a patter of bare feet behind me.

'What's going on, Dindy?' said Pog.

'Mother's ill.'

'Oh. When are we going to have our tea?'

'I don't know.'

'I'm going to go and ask Krishna.'

'Better not. Everyone's busy with Mother. We don't want to get into any more trouble.'

'*I'm* not in trouble,' said Pog, looking horribly pleased with himself. 'You are.'

I wanted to shake him, but I knew he was right. '*Look after Pog,*' Shanti had said, so I decided that I'd better do just that.

'Tea won't be long,' I said. 'Let's go and play with your train set.'

Pog looked at me suspiciously.

'You don't like my train set. You always say it's boring.'

'I don't mind for once. You can be the driver. I'll do the other stuff.'

I started towards his bedroom, which was further away from the front door than mine, but he was going in the other direction, towards Mother's bedroom, and the rooms beyond.

'No, Pog!' I hissed after him. 'We've got to stay down here!'

'But my train's still set up in the drawing room,' he said. 'Daddy was playing with me on Sunday.'

His lower lip was pushed out. I could see that he was ready to make a scene.

'All right,' I said unwillingly, 'but we'll have to be quiet.'

Pog started tiptoeing down the corridor, then he got bored with going slowly, and ran the rest of the way, straight past Mother's bedroom door, to the drawing room beyond. I followed as quietly as I could.

Pog's little railway was set up on a low table in the bay window. I'd never liked it. It was something Pog had always done with Daddy, who had had the same set when he was child. I knew without anyone telling me that girls weren't supposed to like trains. Seeing Daddy and Pog together, having fun with it, had always made me feel left out.

I realized, once we were in the drawing room, that I was glad to be there after all, because we were near Mother's room and I could hear a bit of what was going on. I left the door ajar, and while I stood beside the table, half-heartedly pushing the signals backwards and forwards, and watching Pog set the engines carefully on to the track, I was straining my ears to listen.

At last I heard the bedroom door open and click shut again. Daddy and Dr Kumar had come out into the corridor.

'I'm afraid so,' Dr Kumar was saying. 'An intestinal blockage. A bad one. Possibly caused by a parasite infestation. Has she been unwell for some time?'

'She's been complaining for months. More than a year, in fact. But Dr Dysart . . .'

Dr Kumar cleared his throat.

'Hm. Not an easy thing to diagnose. And she's been using alcohol to dull the symptoms, I suppose.'

'Yes!' Daddy sounded eager. 'That must be why . . . She's not really one of those – you know.'

'An alcoholic.'

'Exactly. Not one of those. So we've just got to deal with this – this parasite, whatever it is, and she'll be her old self. Is that right?'

'In the long term, possibly. But for now, she needs an operation. Urgently.'

'Oh! Can it wait till Friday? The truck's gone down to Cochin. I can take her down to the little hospital in Munnar once it's back.'

'It can't wait that long. It can't wait until tomorrow. It's a question of hours.'

'Dindy!' said Pog. 'Hurry up. You've got to change the points.'

I put my finger over my mouth.

'Shh! They'll hear!'

'I suppose I'll have to do it myself,' Pog said, in his usual voice. 'Girls are useless at trains.'

At last he shut up and I could go back to listening.

'You know that I can't operate without the patient's permission,' Dr Kumar was saying.

'No, no. Of course not. But what about Dr Dysart? If I sent an urgent message . . .'

'His ship left port yesterday. He'll be out at sea by now.'

'And you really think this operation is necessary?'

'I know it is. Without immediate surgery, Mrs Fraser will not survive a week. Gangrene may already be setting in.'

'My God! But look here, Kumar, this isn't a hospital! How can you operate here?'

'With a great deal of help from everyone. Get your cook to boil water. Plenty of it. I'll need clean sheets. It's just as well I never go anywhere without my emergency surgical kit. I'll have to have assistance with the ether. What about the ayah? Do you trust her?'

'Shanti? Yes. She's first rate.'

'You'd better go in and talk to your wife, Mr Fraser. I can't tell you in plainer words. Her life depends on an immediate operation.'

'*Dindy!*' said Pog. 'You're not concentrating! I told you to bring up the guard's van.' When I didn't move, he looked up at me. 'You've gone a funny colour.'

'It's Mother. She's ill.'

'She's always ill.'

'No, really, really ill. Dr Kumar's says he's got to cut her open.'

'That's silly, Dindy. She won't let him. She doesn't like him.'

'If he doesn't, Dr Kumar says she's going to die.'

Pog's mouth fell open, and his eyes were round.

'She can't die. She's not old enough.'

'That's got nothing to do with it.'

Pog's lip began to tremble.

'I don't want Mummy to die! She mustn't!'

His voice was loud and wailing.

'Shut *up!*' I said, suddenly furious with him. 'I *told* you. We've got to be quiet!'

I was about to grab his hand and haul him back down to our end of the bungalow, when I heard Mother's door open again.

'She's agreed,' Daddy said. He sounded hoarse. 'And she wants Shanti with her. Shanti's the only – I mean, she trusts Shanti, I'm glad to say.'

'Good.' Dr Kumar seemed to hesitate. 'But look here, Mr Fraser, I must warn you that this kind of surgery is always tricky, and in these circumstances, away from hospital, in a makeshift operating theatre, it won't be easy.'

'I know what you're saying,' said Daddy. 'No need to spell it out. You can rest assured that if anything goes wrong I'll see to it that no blame attaches to you. Now, what do we have to do?'

'I presume you have a long table in your dining room?' Dr Kumar said briskly. 'Is there a decent light above it? Good. Get your people to roll up any rugs, and remove them and any pictures from the walls. Take out the chairs, and swab the floor and table with Dettol. We need to make the room as sterile as we can.'

Chapter Nine

I didn't want to listen to what was going on any more. I needed to get as far away from everything and everyone as possible.

'We can't stay in here,' I said to Pog. 'We'll have to go back to our rooms.'

Pog scowled at me, then kicked the leg of the table so hard that a whole row of carriages toppled sideways and slid off the tracks.

'It's no fun doing the railway without Daddy, anyway,' he said.

He started towards the drawing-room door, but I called him back. I could see that the corridor was full of people. Krishna and Sunderam were staggering out of the dining room, carrying the carpet between them. Shanti was hurrying into it, a pile of sheets in her arms. Even Ram Lal had been summoned from the gate, and was walking towards the dining room with a mop in one hand and a bucket in the other, trying not to let the water slop over.

'We'll have to go out through the French windows,' I told Pog.

'They're locked.'

'I know where the key is.'

He looked shocked.

'We're not allowed to play with keys.'

'It's not playing. We're being good. We're keeping out of everyone's way.'

The curtains that covered the French windows at night were drawn back. I felt behind them. The key was on a hook halfway up the wooden frame.

Pog watched with interest while I slid it into the lock and turned it. The door opened.

'Come on,' I said.

He hung back.

'We can't go out now. We've had our baths. It's tea-time. We never go into the garden in our pyjamas.'

I suddenly felt sorry for him. He looked little and helpless and upset.

'It's all right, Pog. We'll stay on the veranda. We'll turn the chairs over and make a little house under them. You like that game.'

'No. It's getting dark. I want Shanti.'

'She's busy.'

'I *need* her.'

'I'm here. I'm looking after you.'

'No, you're not. You're making me go outside and be naughty again. I want my tea. I'm going to go to the dining room and see if Krishna's got it ready.'

'No!' I grabbed his arm. 'We can't go to the dining room.'

He was trying to shake me off.

'You're horrid, Dindy. I hate you! Everything's all your fault.'

I felt as if he'd hit me with a hammer.

Was everything my fault? Perhaps it was. Perhaps Mother had got so ill because I'd made her so angry. Perhaps she was going to die, and I'd be the one who'd killed her, and no one would ever forgive me, especially Daddy.

I sat down on the floor, put my head on my knees, and began to cry.

After a while, I felt Pog's hand shaking my shoulder.

'Don't cry, Dindy. I don't like it when you cry.'

His own voice was wobbling.

'*Look after Pog*,' Shanti had said.

I pulled my hand across my nose and sniffed hard. Pog was right about one thing. We did need to have our tea.

'We won't play on the veranda, then,' I said. 'We'll

just go round to the kitchen and see if Krishna's there.'

'That's a good idea, Dindy.' I could tell that Pog was trying to be generous.

He put his hand in mine, and we went out through the French windows. It was getting dark, and from the valley below I could hear the evening hymns being sung to the god Vishnu, and the temple bells ringing. They reminded me that I ought to be praying myself.

'Please, God, don't let Mother die,' I whispered.

'Why are you whispering?' said Pog. 'What are you talking about?'

'Nothing.'

It was odd, being outside in our pyjamas. The veranda only stretched to the end of the bungalow's side wall. After that, we had to walk along a gravel path that ran round the back of the house to the kitchen. I could feel the sharp little stones through the thin soles of my slippers.

We'd hardly ever come round here. Krishna didn't like us hanging round the kitchen.

The back door was half open. I looked inside. No one was there. At the far end of the kitchen was the small serving room, with the dining room beyond. The door into it was tight shut but even the sight of it made me shudder. I couldn't hear anything, but I couldn't bear to be so close to what was going on in there. I wanted to get away at once.

'This is no good,' I started to say, and I turned to back out of the kitchen, but Krishna had appeared silently behind me, blocking the way.

'What are you children doing here? You should be in your rooms.'

'We haven't had our tea,' Pog said aggressively. He

was trying to sound grown-up and bossy again. This time, I felt grateful to him.

'I know, my dears,' said Krishna. 'It's all ready, on a tray. I didn't know where you were. Let's go to Pog's bedroom. I'll bring it to you.'

I was used to Krishna being grumpy and sounding cross. He'd never called us his 'dears' before. It should have made me feel better, but actually it made me feel worse.

'Come,' he said. 'We'll go round through the garden.'

To my amazement, he bent down and picked Pog up. I thought Pog would struggle. He usually hated being picked up and treated like a baby. But being held by Krishna was so unexpected that he didn't say a word. He looked almost funny, trying to appear dignified, and holding himself stiffly in Krishna's arms, but I didn't feel like laughing.

In Pog's bedroom, Krishna fussed around, lifting the toy soldiers off the low table and pulling up our little chairs. Then he disappeared, and came back a moment later with the tray. There were boiled eggs in egg cups, slices of bread and butter, a pot of jam, and glasses of milk. He set everything down, and stood back to watch us eat.

Pog drank all his milk down in one go, leaving a creamy rim round his mouth, but I suddenly didn't feel hungry at all. I watched while Pog smashed the shell on the top of his egg with his spoon, picked the bits off, then pushed the spoon in too hard, making the yolk run down the side of the egg cup. I picked up my own spoon, and put it down again.

'I don't want any tea after all, thank you,' I said.

From the far end of the bungalow, I heard running footsteps, and Sunderam calling out, 'Krishna! Where are you? More boiling water! Quickly!'

Krishna hurried out.

'Can I eat your bread and butter, Dindy?' asked Pog. His mouth was crammed so full of his own last slice that I could hardly understand him.

'Take it.' I pushed my plate towards him.

'I like having tea in here,' he said, grabbing a piece of my bread. 'You can play at the same time.'

He'd pulled a box of farm animals off the shelf beside the table, and was starting to arrange them round his plate.

Then he started on his *Diddy daddy* song, spraying crumbs around. He'd be in his own world for ages. I wouldn't have to think about him any more.

I stood up and went to my own bedroom.

If Mother dies, it'll all be my own fault, I kept saying to myself. *Don't let her die. Please, God, don't let her.*

I needed to feel safe and small. I wriggled under my bed, curled myself into a ball and lay there for a long time.

Chapter Ten

Chapter Ten

I must have been very tired, because I think I fell asleep. Anyway, I didn't hear anything until the springs above my head creaked as someone sat down on my bed. I thought it must be Pog, so I scrambled out, only to see Daddy sitting there, his head in his hands.

The look of him, so tired and beaten down, shocked me, and I forgot how afraid of him I'd been.

'Mother!' I whispered. 'Is she . . .'

He put out one arm and pulled me towards him.

'Mother's going to be fine. She had to have an operation but she'll get better soon.'

'I know about the operation. I heard Dr Kumar talk to you about it. He did it in the dining room.'

'He saved her life. Why old Dysart never suspected . . . Old-fashioned, I suppose. Mother's back in her own bed now. She needs rest.'

Everything welled up inside me.

'Oh, Daddy. I'm sorry, I know it was all my fault. I can't – I didn't . . .'

He pulled me closer.

'Hey, what's all this? What's your fault? No, don't cry.'

'It was because I went out with Pog. She was so cross. She shouted at Dr Kumar, and said all those bad things, and that's what made her ill.'

'Sweetheart.'

He put his hand under my chin to lift my face.

'You didn't make Mother ill. She's been unwell ever since we came to India. She's had these worms in her stomach, and . . .'

I clapped my hands over my mouth.

'*Worms? Inside* her?' I wanted to be sick. 'Is that why she's been so cross and tired and why we never have lessons any more?'

He looked surprised.

'You haven't been having any lessons?'

'No. Not since a long time before Christmas. And is it the worms that are making her drink gin all the time?'

Daddy bit his lip.

'Yes, I expect – I think so.'

He was staring at the floor. I took a deep breath.

There were things I needed to get out of the way.

'Aren't you angry with me, Daddy, for going outside the compound and taking Pog?'

He seemed to come back from far way.

'What? Oh yes, that was naughty, darling. You shouldn't have done it. Why did you run off like that, anyway?'

I couldn't believe how calm he was. He didn't sound angry at all. I started to feel braver and took a deep breath.

'There was nothing to do, and Mother was in her room, and we weren't supposed to make a noise because she was resting, and Pog was being really, really annoying. He wanted to play Going to England, but it's babyish, the way he does it, so I – so I said, "Let's go somewhere properly. Let's go down to the river," and once I'd said it, well, it sort of had to happen.'

'I see.'

'And then there was a snake in the tea bushes, and the boys by the stream, and Nikhil, and we heard about the rogue tusker, and we went to the mahout, and there was this boy called Silveraj.'

I stopped. He didn't seem to be listening.

'How old are you, Dindy?' he said.

I was shocked.

'Don't you know how old I am? I'm nine.'

'When I was nine, I was running round the moors of Ayrshire, falling out of trees and damming up streams with my older brother. And playing with all the other boys at school.'

He had turned his head and was looking out of the window, although there was nothing to see because it was quite dark by now.

'But I haven't got an older brother, Daddy, or a sister. There's only Pog. And he's . . .'

'Too young. I know.'

He'd turned back and was looking at me. It was odd, but I felt as if he was seeing me for the first time.

'It hasn't been much fun for you here, has it? No friends, no school, nowhere to go, nothing to do. It won't be much longer now. We'll be going home soon. Just another month or so, and . . .'

I'd known this was coming. It was the moment I'd dreaded.

'No, Daddy! I love it here! I don't want to go and live anywhere else! I don't want to leave India ever! And I can't manage without Shanti. I'll – I'll die!'

It was as if, by saying her name, I'd called to her, because she came into the room at that moment.

'Mem Sahib is sleeping,' she said to Daddy. 'Looks quite comfortable now. Dr Sahib wants to speak to you.'

Daddy stood up and dropped a kiss on the top of my head.

'Isn't it past your bedtime, darling? Why were you under your bed, anyway?'

I opened my mouth and shut it again. There was no point in telling him how scared I'd been. I couldn't understand what had happened. Daddy hadn't been angry with me at all.

Anyway, he was talking to Shanti now.

'Thank you, Shanti. I don't know how Dr Kumar would have managed the operation without you. You'd have made an excellent hospital nurse. And I don't know what would have become of my whole family all these years without you either, for that matter.'

Shanti flushed and waggled her head in thanks. Daddy went to the door, but instead of going out, he stood there, one hand on the doorknob.

'By the way, I spoke to Mr Richardson about you. You've heard of the Richardsons? They're on the next plantation up the valley. The company have asked him to stay on after independence. His wife's expecting a baby in the new year. There's a job for you there if you want it.'

I curled my fingers till my hands were balled so tight that my nails dug into my palms.

She can't! I thought. *She mustn't go to another family! She's ours. Mine!*

I was hating Mrs Richardson's baby already. But Shanti was shaking her head.

'Thank you, sir, but I've been talking to my brother. He wants me stay with him in Munnar. His wife is poorly and they need my help with the children. And

Nikhil can live with me there. He'll be closer to his school.'

'Nikhil, of course,' said Daddy. 'But what about his school fees?'

'I've saved what I can from my wages,' said Shanti, looking proud, 'and there is a money lender in Munnar.'

'We can't have you going to a money lender,' said Daddy. 'You can leave Nikhil's school fees to me. I'll set up something for him with the bank here. It's the least we can do after all you've done for us.'

And then he had gone.

A huge smile had spread over Shanti's face, but she looked too surprised to say anything.

She looks so pleased it must mean she doesn't mind us going at all, I thought, and my heart shrivelled at the thought. *She doesn't care.*

'Why don't you want to work for the Richardsons, Shanti?' I asked her, my voice sounding small.

She picked up my hairbrush and started sweeping it gently through my hair in the way that I'd always found so comforting.

'It's time I looked after my own family, Dindy. And anyway –' she paused – 'I don't want to get to love any more children, and see them leave India, and know that they'll forget all about old Shanti when they're far away in England.'

'Do you mean me, Shanti? And Pog? About loving us, I mean?'

'You know I do.'

I flung my arms round her.

'I'll never forget you, as long as I live. I promise. You're the best person in the whole world to me.'

I climbed into bed and she tucked me in, as she had done every night ever since I could remember. And then she kissed me, and pulled the curtains, turned the light out and went.

I couldn't go back to sleep straight away. Shanti had left a gap between the curtains, and I could look up at the crescent moon, as thin as a fingernail, and the stars studding the night sky.

There'll be the moon and stars in England too, I suppose, I thought, and then I fell asleep.

Chapter Eleven

The weeks that followed passed horribly quickly. Daddy sent for the tea truck the day after Mother's operation, and took her down to the little hospital in Munnar, where Dr Kumar could look after her better. We were supposed to visit her, but no one found the time to take us.

News came through that Daddy had been offered a good job in Edinburgh. It was something to do with Scotland's forests. We wouldn't live in London, like Mother had wanted, but at least Edinburgh was a city, and there would be shops and cinemas and the things she liked. Daddy would have to travel about sometimes in the Highlands, but he'd love that, and Pog and I would go to school. I'd have to wear a tartan skirt, Daddy said, and plait my hair in pigtails.

It was horrible when the packers came. They brought dozens of tea chests and put all our things into them. Sunderam and Shanti were busy all day, sorting and packing, and no one had time for us.

I was scared of leaving India and going to England. It felt as if we were going to jump out of a world of light and warmth and beautiful things, and plunge down into a big black hole. A cold one.

I don't think I could have borne those last days if it hadn't been for Daddy. Every night, before we went to bed, he'd sit down with us and tell us about the fun we'd have on the ship, and the things we'd do in Scotland.

Pog believed every word, and got wildly excited, strutting around being the driver of the *Flying*

Scotsman, the huge steam engine that would pull our train from London to Edinburgh, then kicking an imaginary football around.

I was suspicious. I didn't think that Daddy was lying, exactly, but I didn't think he was telling the whole truth either. I knew he was trying to make us feel better about leaving India.

The children at the school mightn't like me, I'd tell myself. *I don't know how to do plaits. I won't like the cold. I'll miss Sunderam, and Krishna, and Ram Lal. I won't be able to live without Shanti.*

Bit by bit, though, Daddy's stories made me feel a little bit excited too. There would be snow in Scotland, and castles, and cartoon films, and my cousins. I'd learn to play netball and the piano. One day, Daddy promised, he'd take us to Paris and we'd climb the Eiffel Tower.

I was sitting in my empty room on the day before we left, resting a piece of paper on my knee and trying to draw a picture to take to Mother. We were going to collect her from the hospital on the way down to the port, where our ship was already docked.

Shanti put her head round the door.

'Someone's here to see you,' she said.

I looked up, surprised.

'Go and see. He's waiting on the veranda.'

Nikhil was standing awkwardly outside the French windows, looking embarrassed.

'I've come to say goodbye,' he said.

'Oh.' I felt embarrassed too.

He hesitated.

'Good luck in England, on the journey and everything.'

We'd slipped into Malalayam, and as the familiar words ran off my tongue, I realized that I wouldn't have anyone except Pog to speak it with in England.

Nikhil was already turning away.

'Don't go!' I said. 'I want to say sorry.'

'What for?'

'For taking your mother away. I've thought about it a lot since – since that day.'

He shook his head.

'You didn't really take her away. And if you did it wasn't your fault. She needed the work. If she hadn't had this job, I wouldn't have been able to go to school. Your father said he'd pay my fees till I've finished school. He won't need to, and I don't want him to. I've applied for a scholarship, and I'm going to make sure I get it. I don't mind working hard. I'm going to be a doctor, like Dr Kumar. Will you tell your father that?'

I nodded fiercely. I was really impressed.

'I'll tell him. I wish I could do that. Be a doctor, I mean.'

'You can, if you study hard enough. Girls can be doctors too.'

We stood there, saying nothing.

'Anyway,' Nikhil said gruffly, 'My mother liked working for you. She really loves you. More than me, I sometimes think.'

'I don't believe that. I don't think she does.'

He grinned suddenly, and a wedge of his thick black hair flopped down over his forehead. As he swept it back. I realized how handsome he was.

'Actually, you're right,' he said. 'She's got to love me more than you. She's my mother, after all.'

'My mother doesn't love me.'

'I bet she does.'

'No, really. She's always cross. She never wants to be with me. She tells me all the time to go away and stop bothering her.'

He thought about this for a moment.

'Perhaps she's jealous,' he said at last. 'Maybe she thinks you should love her but you only really love my mother. Perhaps it'll be different when you're in England, when you're with her all the time.'

'It's Scotland, not England,' I said automatically, but I'd understood what he'd said. I'd think about it later, and wonder if he was right.

'It'll be different in Eng– Scotland,' he said again, and I knew he was trying to be kind.

'I know,' I said with a heavy sigh. 'It won't be the same at all.'

'I wish I could go with you,' he said suddenly, a light flaring in his eyes.

'Why? It's all cold, and dark, and everything smells of soot.'

'We did a poem at school,' he said. 'About London. It starts "Earth has not anything to show more fair".'

The English words sounded funny in the middle of the Malayalam and I couldn't quite understand them, but I didn't like to say so.

'Tell you what,' I said. 'Let's swap. You go to England and I'll stay here.'

We both laughed.

'You're different from the others, Dindy,' he said, suddenly serious.

'What others?'

'Other British. That day, when you came out and

went down to the river, you didn't look at us like most white people do. I was a bit angry with you. I'm sorry.'

I shuddered. I didn't want to remember that day, and how it had ended.

'I'm going to come back,' I said, making a sudden decision. 'I'm going to come back to India. Don't forget that, Nikhil. I mean it. When I grow up, I'm going to come back home.'

Glossary

Ayah   An ayah is a nanny who lives with a family and looks after the children.

Bearer   A manservant.

Mahout   A man who is specially trained to work with elephants.

Sahib   This means 'Sir' or 'Mister'. European women in India were often called **Mem sahib**.

Tusker   A tusker is an animal with tusks. It is often used to describe a male elephant with big tusks.

Elizabeth Laird

The Fastest Boy in the World

Turn the page to read an extract

Chapter One

In my dreams I'm always running, running, running. Sometimes my feet fly over the ground and I'm sure that if I could just go a little bit faster I'd take off and fly like an eagle. Sometimes my legs feel as heavy as tree trunks, but I know that I must go on and reach the finishing line whatever it costs.

I've been running almost since I was a toddler. As soon as I could toddle, I'd stagger after my father as fast as my little legs would take me when he set out for the market on our donkey.

'Solomon! Come back!' my mother would shout. I wouldn't listen, so she'd have to run after me, snatch me up and laugh with me all the way home.

That was how my childhood began. And I can remember, as clearly as anything, the night when everything changed.

I was eleven years old. At least, I think I was eleven. In the countryside in Ethiopia, nobody takes much notice of how old you are.

It was the end of the day, and the door of our house was firmly shut. It always made me shiver to think of the night outside. Not just because it was dark and cold, but because there might be a hyena or two, lurking in the darkness, or, even worse, something – demonish.

I'll have to explain what our family home was like, in case you have never been to Ethiopia. It was round, like most other people's houses up there in our cool highlands, and it had a thatched roof that went up to a point. There was only one room, with the fire burning away in the middle. It got a bit smoky, but it kept us warm and gave a glowing light. There was a screen at one end, and our animals lived behind it – at night, that is. In the daytime, of course, they were out grazing.

Anyway, that evening Ma was stirring the pot of stew that was cooking over the fire. The smell was so good it was making me feel very hungry.

'How old am I, Ma?' I said suddenly. I don't know what put the idea into my head.

'Let me see,' she said vaguely, dropping another pinch of red-hot pepper into the pot. I could tell she wasn't listening.

Abba (that's what we called my father) *was*

listening, though. He had just come in from his work out on our farm. He sat down on a little stool beside the fire, and I could see he was as hungry as I was.

'You were born the year the harvest was so bad, and we had to borrow all that money from your uncle,' he said.

Ma looked reproachfully at him.

Abba blinked, and looked a bit guilty.

'I wasn't thinking,' he said quietly. 'It was Hailu who was born that year.'

Hailu was my older brother, but he died when he was little. Ma always sighs when anyone reminds her of him.

Abba shot her an understanding look, then he scratched his head.

'Oh no, I remember now,' he said. 'You were born the year the magician came and turned my stick into a wand of gold.'

I loved it when Abba was in his teasing mood. Konjit, my little sister, had been picking up the unburnt ends of twigs and throwing them on to the fire, while twisting a bit of hair over her forehead at the same time. She only ever seems to use one hand for anything useful. The other one is permanently fiddling with her hair. Now, though, she stopped for a whole long minute.

'Oh!' she said, her big brown eyes as round as the buttons on Grandfather's cotton jacket. 'A gold wand? Where is it?'

I nudged her, just to show that I knew she was being silly, then had to pull her upright in case she toppled over into the fire.

'It turned back into a stick again, just like that,' Abba said, giving me a sly look. 'Anyway, it wasn't that year. You were born just at the time when Twisty Horn had twins, only they didn't turn out to be calves but a couple of chickens. You should have seen them! They went flapping about all over the place.'

Everyone laughed, and even Grandfather, who had been sitting on the clay bench that ran right round the wall of the house, made a sort of rusty, wheezing sound that meant that he was laughing too, but Konjit didn't even smile. She looked quite shocked.

'Cows can't have chickens for babies, Abba,' she said seriously. 'Everyone knows that.'

She falls for it every time.

Just at that moment, a whiffling snort came from the stable behind the screen of sticks. I knew it was

Twisty Horn, and not Long Tail or Big Hoof. I know the sound of all our animals. I can tell our donkey (her name is Lucky) from all the other donkeys at the market just by the way she brays. I know our three dogs too, of course, but they don't come into the house with us. Their job is to stay outside and guard our farm. They pretty much look after themselves.

'You're quite right, darling. Cows only have calves,' said Abba, pulling Konjit sideways so that she could lean against his arm. I could tell his teasing mood was over. He was too tired for much when the evening came. He'd been out working all day on the farm.

'Supper's ready,' Ma said at last. She fetched out the big enamel tray and laid a huge round piece of pancake bread on it. (Our bread is called 'injera', and it's soft and thin and delicious.) Then she scooped spoonfuls of stew from the pot and set them out in front of each of our places.

Grandfather stood up and walked over to join us by the fire. I waited expectantly.

Five, I said to myself.

I counted the steps he was taking, and, sure enough, his knees cracked like breaking sticks at the fifth step.

(I like doing that – guessing numbers, I mean. It's a private game I play with myself, and with my friend Marcos, when he's in the right mood.)

Grandfather sat down on the little stool that Abba had pulled up for him.

'Solomon's eleven,' he said.

I'd forgotten by now that I'd asked about my age. It was my job to take the bowl and the little jug of water round so that everyone could wash their hands before they ate, yet I was too hungry to think about anything but food.

No one said much while we were eating, but when we'd had enough Grandfather sat back on his stool and said again, more thoughtfully this time, 'Solomon's eleven.'

I thought his mind was wandering, but it wasn't. He suddenly squared his shoulders, pulled the end of his thick white shawl away from his neck, as if he was too hot, and said, for the third time, 'Eleven. Quite old enough. We'll go tomorrow.'

My parents went quiet. Ma froze with her hand halfway up to her mouth. Abba had pulled his little tooth-cleaning stick from his inside pocket. He froze too.

'Go where?' whispered Konjit. She didn't dare

speak up in front of Grandfather. I knew she was burning to add, 'Wherever it is, can I come too?' but she would never have been so disrespectful. I was glad she'd asked the question, though, because I was burning to ask it too.

'To Addis Ababa,' said Grandfather.